AN XAVION AND JAMIESON
TIME-OUT ADVENTURE

NEVER TALK TO RAVENS

M.L. FLURRY

TABLE OF CONTENTS

"IT'S LIKE TRYING TO PIN DOWN A KANGAROO ON A TRAMPOLINE."

—SID WADDELL, BRITISH SPORTS COMMENTATOR

CHAPTER ONE

KANGAROOS AND FLAPJACKS

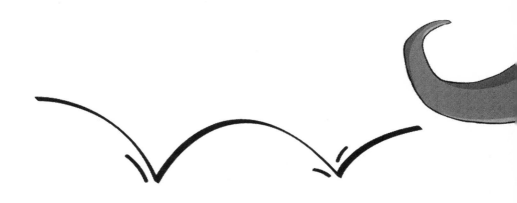

The kangaroo kept tugging on Xavion's sleeve. Xavion was sitting in the shade of the time-out tree. All he wanted to do was sleep. That way, he could forget all about time-out.

But the kangaroo wouldn't leave him alone.

Perfect, Xavion thought. *That's*

just perfect. What a day.

The day was not off to a good start. And it was all because of his big feet. Well, his big feet and his big mouth.

Xavion usually got along with everyone at school. He could make his best friend Ty laugh so hard at lunch that milk squirted out of his nose. He could name all the states and all the capitals. He could even twirl a basketball on his index finger for twenty-nine Mississippis. And he never, ever got in trouble.

Well, almost never.

Earlier, two of Xavion's classmates had been teasing him about his big feet.

Again.

Xavion's feet had almost doubled in size during the summer. His mom said he would grow into them, but for now, they were always in his way. And, it seemed, in everyone else's way, too. His classmates and sometimes even teachers tripped over his feet.

The one good thing was that his feet made him a really good jumper — which didn't seem to matter much when the name-calling began.

"Hey flapjack!" The first shout had come from Austin. No surprise there. If you wanted to find trouble, Austin was your man. The teachers could shout his name faster than almost any other.

"You got a ZIP code for those feet?" That shout had come from Chris.

Chris didn't always pick on Xavion. When no one else was around, Xavion and Chris played one-on-one. Chris never talked about Xavion's feet then. Maybe because Xavion usually won.

"Somebody call Bigfoot." That was Austin again. "Tell him we found his shoes."

Xavion didn't mind even one or two names. Some of them were even funny. He did mind getting laughed at by Austin, Chris, and the others who always seemed to appear at just the wrong time.

First, Xavion had told Mrs. Barnes, his homeroom teacher. That helped a little. For a while, Austin and Chris whispered the names instead of yelling them. Of course, they also added "tattletale" and "snitch" to the names they whispered.

Xavion knew he should ignore Austin and Chris. He tried taking deep breaths like his mom said. He thought about telling Mrs. Barnes again.

"HEY SASQUATCH!"

Austin shouted that day at recess.

Austin, Chris and a dozen or so of Xavion's classmates surrounded Xavion.

"No snow today. You can take those skis off."

On a scale of one to ten, Xavion thought, *not funny.*

But everybody else thought Austin was hilarious. Chris laughed so hard that he snorted.

Xavion's face reddened. Then his ears. Then his nose.

"It's Rudolph, the big-foot reindeer," Austin said.

14

Even funnier. The kids laughed louder and louder and louder until …

Enough, Xavion thought.

Xavion didn't take a deep breath. He didn't look for a teacher. He didn't walk away. Instead, he found himself calling Austin "four-eyes" at the top of his lungs.

Four-eyes? thought Xavion. *Seriously? Who says four-eyes anymore?*

A stunned silence rightly fell over

the crowd. When he had yelled four-eyes, Xavion had pumped up the volume to an eardrum bursting level. Xavion had never yelled that loud before. That much noise meant a teacher would soon appear. Even worse, two violations of playground protocol had occurred.

First, you never called Austin anything except "Austin." And you especially didn't call him four-eyes at the top of your lungs.

Second, you never teased someone else about something you shared. Sarah, the third-grader who lisped, would never tease another lisper. Xavion wore glasses but only to read. Even though he didn't wear glasses all the time, he had technically violated that rule when he yelled four-eyes.

This was uncharted territory. Austin stood motionless and speechless, a condition that would not last. Chris watched Austin. In fact, everyone's eyes were on Austin when a tall figure appeared.

Mrs. Barnes.

The crowd parted. A crow cawed from the time-out tree.

CHAPTER TWO

JUMPIN' JAMIESON

Bad move, thought Xavion. Maybe I should have taken that deep breath after all.

Now, here he was, sitting by himself under the time-out tree. He couldn't run or wrestle or play basketball — his favorite — for an entire week. Basketball was his best sport. He could jump super high.

Xavion was stuck in time-out

— five recesses in a row. If his mom found out, he knew she wouldn't let him go to the annual carnival that weekend. Xavion was aggravated and bored and so, so sleepy.

He decided to take a nap. But every time he drifted off, that kangaroo tugged his sleeve.

"Did I see a kangaroo?" Xavion finally asked himself. He jumped up, a little frightened.

Kangaroos didn't usually hang around the playground. In fact, kangaroos didn't usually live in his town.

Now, a kangaroo was tugging his sleeve.

"Sorry to bother you, mate," the kangaroo said. "You're hard to wake up, but I need your help."

"Wh-wh-wh-where did you come from?" Xavion asked.

The kangaroo didn't answer. The kangaroo was already gone.

Xavion rubbed his eyes. Had he seen a real, live kangaroo? Then a strange shadow bounced across the playground. He looked up to see the kangaroo plummeting feet first from the sky.

"Hurry!" the kangaroo shouted. "Be a good bloke and grab some rocks."

Xavion did.

The kangaroo seemed to disappear, leaving only his shadow again.

More kangaroo words fell from the sky. "Now when I land, stand on my feet," the kangaroo yelled, as he soared past the top of the tree. "Then put the rocks in my pouch."

Xavion spotted a bright orange pack around the kangaroo's waist.

When the kangaroo landed, Xavion jumped on top of his feet and put the rocks in the outside pocket. The kangaroo's feet were even bigger than Xavion's. Xavion thought nobody had bigger feet than he did. Xavion hoped that Austin and Chris wouldn't make fun of the kangaroo's feet.

"That's better," the kangaroo said, "much better." The rocks helped keep him from jumping so much. The kangaroo gathered a few more rocks to be safe.

"Who are you?" Xavion asked again.

"I have left my spaceship to invade your planet," the kangaroo said. Xavion thought the kangaroo wanted to sound like the space aliens he had seen in movies. **"Now, take me to your leader."**

"You're not from another planet," Xavion said, laughing. The kangaroo didn't seem so scary after all. "I know you're a kangaroo. I meant, 'What's your name?' And what are you doing here? Besides, I can't take you to my leader or anywhere else. I'm in time-out."

"The name is Edward Jamieson Goodday, Jr.," the kangaroo said. "Call me Jamieson. Or Jumpin' Jay. That's what my mates call me because I'm a really good jumper."

A good jumper, thought Xavion. *We'll see who's the best jumper.*

"My name's Xavion."

"Pleasure to meet you, Xavion. Now, can you help me get back Down Under?"

"Down where?" asked Xavion.

"The outback, mate," said Jamie-son.

Xavion stared at him.

"Australia?" said Jamieson. "You know, the country?"

"Oh," Xavion said. "I'm sorry to tell you this, but that's a long way from here. Can't you go back the same way you came?"

"That's the problem," said Jamieson. "You see, I can't without your help. I was playing basketball when—"

"Xavion," Mrs. Barnes called. "Wake up. Time for class."

Xavion wondered why Mrs. Barnes thought he was sleeping. "Can you stay here until tomorrow?" Xavion asked. He wanted to hear Jamieson's story. And it was making time-out kind of fun. "Or will you accidentally bounce away?"

Jamieson agreed to stay. "I've been jumping so long from so high that it was hard to stop," Jamieson said. "I'm fine now. But my birthday is on Sunday, and I need to be home by then."

The two walked toward the school building where Mrs. Barnes was lining up the class.

"Plus, there's a grand prize waiting for me," Jamieson said. "We'll need lots of trampolines. Will you help me?"

Xavion said he would help, although he wasn't sure how and didn't have even one trampoline.

Since it was only Monday, he had plenty of time to plan. He wondered what the prize was, but there was no time to ask. He put a few more rocks in Jamieson's orange pack, in case he was still too bouncy. Xavion gave Jamieson his only dollar to buy a snack.

"Until tomorrow," Jamieson said.
"Until tomorrow," Xavion agreed.

CHAPTER THREE

BEWARE THE RAVENS

Xavion could see Mrs. Barnes looking at him, puzzled. *She has no idea why I'm happy about time-out*, Xavion thought.

Xavion sat in the usual time-out spot under the big oak tree in the far corner of the playground. He did not see or hear Jamieson anywhere.

Xavion had read about kangaroos

during library hour. He knew that kangaroos liked to sleep during the daytime. Maybe Jamieson was napping. Come to think of it, Xavion felt a little sleepy himself.

That's what he likes to do, Xavion thought when he heard Jamieson call his name. *He likes to wake me up.*

"So, where were we?" Jamieson asked, twirling his whiskers as he thought. "I remember. I was about to tell you how I came to land at your school."

"Wait," said Xavion. He saw the dollar bill he had given Jamieson. It was sticking out of Jamieson's pack. "You didn't spend the dollar. Aren't you hungry?"

"Well..." said Jamieson. He glanced toward the hundred-foot-long row of bushes that ran along the school wall.

"I ate a little snack last night."

The row of bushes was now half as tall as it had been the day before. Green leaves clung to Jamieson's fur.

"I see," Xavion said, smiling. "Looks like there's enough left for your supper. OK, let's hear your story."

"Actually," Jamieson said, "let's watch the movie version instead."

Jamieson pulled two chairs, a DVD player, and a remote control from his orange pack.

Xavion couldn't believe how much stuff was in Jamieson's pack. He also wondered why Jamieson wore his pack the wrong way. Xavion and his friends always wore their packs on their backs.

"It's not a pack. It's a pouch, mate," said Jamieson. "And pouches go in front. My mum even has a built-in pouch. That's where my little brother likes to ride."

He pulled a box of hot popcorn from his pouch. "Popcorn?" he asked.

Some of the rocks in Jamieson's pouch had fallen into the popcorn. Xavion picked out a few rocks and sat back to watch the movie.

The movie was a little confusing. Jamieson called his mom **"mum."** And he never called the other kangaroos neighbors or friends. Instead, he called them his **"mob."** He didn't have a best friend. Instead, he had a **"best mate."** And he talked about ravens, which he said were never to be trusted.

The movie showed Jamieson's mum and dad working in their yard and grilling grass burgers.

were one of Jamieson's favorite meals.

It was a Saturday. Jamieson and his friends were shooting hoops when the ravens flew into town.

"Here comes the good part," Jamieson said.

Xavion concentrated on the movie.

Jamieson knew the ravens were up to something.

"Ignore them," Jamieson's mum had always said. "Ravens are always causing mischief. Once you start talking to them, Jamieson, they will always trick you."

So, Jamieson did ignore them —
for a while.

"Hey, Jamieson," croaked the chief
raven. "How'd you learn to jump so
high?"

Jamieson pretended not to hear
them.

"Hey, Jamieson," squawked another raven. "Bet nobody can jump higher than you."

Jamieson said nothing, but he began to think his mum was wrong. The ravens seemed all right. And he liked what they were saying.

"Nice dunk," the chief raven croaked again. "Did you see that, guys? Bet he could win the grand prize."

Jamieson and his mates turned toward the ravens. Jamieson stopped dribbling.

"What grand prize?" asked Jamieson, trying hard not to sound too interested.

"Did I say 'grand prize'?" the chief raven croaked. "I don't think I said grand prize."

"Grand prize?" another raven said. "I didn't hear you say 'grand prize,' boss. 'Bland mice' maybe. But mice are always bland. That's why I add hot sauce."

The ravens all laughed, flapped, and croaked.

But Jamieson and his friends persisted.

"We all heard you say 'grand prize' and not 'bland mice'," said Jamieson. "So, tell me what the prize is and what I have to do to win."

The chief raven huddled with the other ravens for a long time. Then the chief raven flew down from the tree and landed on Jamieson's basketball.

"So, you want to win the grand prize?" said the chief raven.

"Maybe," said Jamieson.

But he and the chief raven both knew that was a lie. Jamieson definitely wanted to win the grand prize.

"You know," the chief raven said, "you'll have to bounce higher than any kangaroo has ever bounced before."

Jamieson already knew that. What he wanted to know about was the prize.

"Oh, that," the chief raven said. **"How does one million pepperoni pizzas sound?"**

"Wow!" said Jamieson. "That sounds like the best prize ever." His mates all nodded, bounced, and high-fived in agreement. "We'll have pizza forever!"

"Excellent," said the chief raven. "There are just a few details to arrange."

The chief raven pulled a stack of legal-looking papers from beneath his wing and handed Jamieson a pen.

"You'll need to sign here," said the chief raven. "And here... and... here."

Jamieson began signing. He could almost taste the pepperonis.

"What's all this about?" asked Jamieson as he handed the papers and pen back.

"It's a contract saying that you'll do it," the chief raven said. A long pause followed. The chief raven covered his mouth with his wing. He coughed as he spoke. He talked fast.

"And it says that I, the chief raven,

will act as your agent, manager, and trainer," the chief raven mumbled. "And for performing those duties, I will receive half the prize."

"*Half?*" Jamieson said. "**Half the prize? No way am I doing that.**"

The chief raven explained that he and the other ravens had worked on a plan for the jump for months.

"We've earned it," the chief raven said. "**There's no way you can win without us.**"

Jamieson wasn't so sure about that. After all, ravens were not exactly famous for their jumping ability.

"You'll still have plenty of pizzas," the chief raven said. "**We need the best jumper around. Are you in?**"

Jamieson wanted more than any-

thing to try for the prize. He knew he shouldn't talk to the ravens, but he couldn't see the harm in their plan. And Jamieson loved prizes. And he especially loved pepperoni pizza. He didn't want to share the prize with the chief raven, but he would still get half a million pizzas. That would be a lot of pizza.

Jamieson's friends started chanting his name. Then the ravens joined in.

"JAM-IE-SON! JAM-IE-SON! JUMPIN' JAY! JAM-IE-SON!" *they shouted and squawked, louder and louder.*

"OK, I'm in," Jamieson finally said. "When do we start?"

The ravens flapped, croaked, and

circled in excitement. "*Come back tomorrow afternoon,*" the chief raven said. "*We'll have everything set up. You just be ready for the jump of your life.*"

"*And Jamieson,*" said the chief raven, "*whatever you do, don't tell your mum.*"

Xavion looked up to see Mrs. Barnes tapping his arm.

"Time to go back to class, Xavion," said Mrs. Barnes.

Xavion hoped Mrs. Barnes hadn't seen Jamieson, but he was nowhere around.

He's almost as good at hiding as he is at jumping, thought Xavion.

Xavion couldn't wait to hear what happened when Jamieson met the ravens. He worried because Jamieson was here and not in Australia. Something must have gone wrong.

Jamieson, thought Xavion, *probably should have ignored the ravens.*

CHAPTER FOUR

THE BIG JUMP

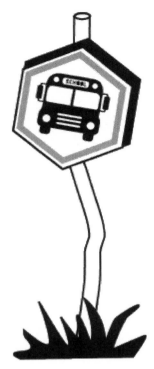

When Xavion got off the bus at school the next morning, he noticed the row of shrubs was completely gone. He didn't see Jamieson, but he figured the kangaroo was still around. From the looks of the disappearing shrubs, Jamieson must have eaten a very big supper. Xavion could hardly wait until recess.

When recess came, Mrs. Barnes walked Xavion to the time-out spot. "Don't worry, Xavion," Mrs. Barnes said. "You'll be able to play with your friends soon."

"Yes, ma'am," said Xavion. He didn't tell her about Jamieson.

"That's right," Austin and Chris piped in. "Don't you worry. We'll be waiting for you."

That did not sound good.

Xavion was getting sleepy waiting for Jamieson. His eyelids had begun to flutter. Then he detected the un-mistakable scent of popcorn and shrubs.

Jamieson handed Xavion another box of popcorn from his pouch.

"Now, where were we?" said Jamieson, picking a few rocks and leaves out of his popcorn.

"Did you ever tell your mom, I mean, mum?" Xavion asked.

"Now, I remember where we were," said Jamieson. He was quiet for a long time. A tear landed on his whiskers. "I did exactly what the ravens wanted. That's where it all went wrong."

Jamieson pulled the remote control from his pouch and started the movie.

Xavion watched the screen.

Jamieson knew that his family suspected something. And why wouldn't they? After all, Jamieson picked jumping beans instead of pepperoni pizza for supper. Jamieson figured the beans would make him jump even higher.

When I win the grand prize, *thought Jamieson,* I'll have pepperoni pizza forever.

Then Jamieson said no when his

dad asked him to go for an evening hop — another one of Jamieson's favorite things. Jamieson said he was too tired, but he actually wanted to save his energy.

Jamieson knew he needed to meet the ravens before his mum and dad asked him too many questions. So, after church the next day, Jamieson skipped lunch. He put on his bounciest shoes, got a few of his best mates, and set out for the basketball court.

"What do you think you're doing?" yelled Jamieson's dad.

Jamieson froze. Game over, he thought. We're caught.

"You can't play basketball without a ball," his dad said as he tossed *him the basketball.*

Close call, *thought Jamieson.*

When they got to the court, Jamieson and his mates could hardly believe their eyes. The ravens must have worked all night. Jamieson had never seen that many trampolines in one place.

A trampoline, just like the one Jamieson's friend had in his back-

yard, stood on the ground. A smaller trampoline sat in the branches of a tree. Jamieson looked up. All he saw were trampolines placed higher and higher in the trees.

"Hey, what's up with all these trampolines?" Jamieson yelled.

The ravens were busy flying trampolines into trees. They hadn't noticed Jamieson and his mates.

The chief raven flew down. He perched on the head of one of Jamieson's best mates.

"Hey Jamieson," the chief raven said. "Glad you could make it. We're almost ready for you."

Then the raven flew away. He didn't explain about the trampolines. He didn't even apologize for

landing on Jamieson's mate's head. Jamieson was beginning to think his mum was right. He shouldn't have talked to the ravens.

"Better eat something," the chief raven yelled down. "It might be a long time before your next meal."

Jamieson wondered why the chief raven said that, but there was no time to ask.

The chief raven tossed down a pepperoni pizza and flew back to the trampolines.

Well, maybe, *thought Jamieson,* the ravens were all right after all.

Sitting in the shade of a big tree, Jamieson and his mates ate pizza. They gazed at more trampolines than they had ever seen. When the ravens finally finished, Jamieson had fallen asleep.

Then the chief raven called Xavion's name. "X-a-vi-on," the raven called. "X-a-vi-on."

Huh? Xavion had no idea how the chief raven knew his name.

"That's not the chief raven calling you, mate," Jamieson said. "That's your teacher. I already stopped the movie. Better hurry. "

Xavion ran to catch up with his class. He hoped Jamieson would finish his story tomorrow.

CHAPTER FIVE

UP, UP AND AWAY

It rained all that night. The next day, rain filled the potholes and mud-died the playground. The red flag in the hall meant no outside recess to-day. Xavion worried.

"You'll still be in time-out," Mrs. Barnes said. "You'll sit in the hall in-stead."

Xavion smiled. Mrs. Barnes looked confused.

"Are you actually enjoying time-out?" Mrs. Barnes asked.

But Xavion didn't say a word.

Although he wasn't sure how, Xavion knew that Jamieson would find him. Xavion was napping at a desk in the hall when Jamieson tapped him on the shoulder.

"We've got to whisper since we're inside," Jamieson said. "Lots of mates around." Jamieson needed to finish telling how he landed in Xavion's playground soon.

It was already Thursday, and Jamieson's birthday was on Sunday. Xavion hoped he would be able to help Jamieson get home.

"I really want to see my mum and dad," Jamieson said, "and even my little brother. And I especially want to get my grand prize."

Jamieson pulled some more popcorn from his pouch and handed it to Xavion.

"Ready?" Jamieson asked as he pulled out the remote control.

Xavion nodded and picked more rocks and leaves out of his popcorn.

"I fast forwarded a little so we could finish," Jamieson said. Then he started the movie.

The jump for the grand prize had already begun.

Jamieson hopped to the base of the first trampoline and took a deep *breath. Here goes, he thought. Then he hopped onto the first trampoline. He bounced there a few times.*

"Now, jump to the trampoline in the lowest branch of the tree," the chief raven croaked.

"Oh-oh-oh -kaaay," Jamieson said. His voice cracked. He was nervous.

After a couple of tries, Jamieson made it. When he glanced down, he felt a little woozy. He had never jumped this high before, and there were lots of trampolines above him. Then stretched between the tips of the two highest trees was a giant rubber band.

That looks like a slingshot, *Jamieson thought*. No way am I going to —

"Don't think," the chief raven yelled, interrupting Jamieson's thoughts. "You're doing great. Just keep bouncing."

So, Jamieson did what the chief raven said. He stopped thinking. And he bounced from one trampoline to another, until he was bouncing way

above the tree tops. There were no trampolines left.

"Did I win the grand prize?" Jamieson yelled. "I set the world record! Woo-hoo!"

Jamieson looked down to see if he could spot the trophy or the pizzas. That was a mistake. Jamieson was so high that his mates looked like baby ants. Jamieson felt dizzy.

"M-m-m-mister R-r-r-raven," Jamieson shouted. He tried to sound brave, but his voice wiggled. "I'm coming down now."

The chief raven flapped up to Jamieson.

"One more jump, and you'll set the record and win the prize," the chief raven said. "You'll never have

to jump this high again."

"Never?" Jamieson asked.

"Nevermore," croaked the raven. "Ready on slingshot one."

Two ravens stretched the rubber band as far as it would go.

"When I count to three, jump to the center of the rubber band," the raven squawked.

Jamieson was in the middle of a very high jump.

"That will be the last jump. Got it?"

"Got it," Jamieson said. He felt re-lieved that he was almost finished.

One more jump, *he thought.* Sure-ly, he could make one more jump. A few seconds later, he heard the chief raven count.

"ONE, TWO, THREE!"

Jamieson jumped toward the rubber band and felt like he would fall forever. Then his feet hit the rubber slingshot.

"Now!" the chief raven croaked. The two ravens stretching the rubber band let go, and Jamieson soared skyward. He rose higher and higher. First, he passed the chief raven.

"See you around, Jamieson," the chief raven croaked. "Or not. Since you're not coming back," he yelled, "we'll take your share of the pizza, too."

Why would he say that? *Jamieson wondered.*

Next, Jamieson blasted by a flock of geese. Then he soared past a black cloud shaped like a dinosaur. Jamieson called for help.

"Helllllllp!"

A family in a hot-air balloon tried to grab his legs but missed. Jamie-

son was going too fast.

Finally, Jamieson reached the top of the sky. The tips of his ears had entered outer space when he finally stopped rising.

Jamieson looked down to find a landing spot, but he didn't see any trampolines.

In fact, he didn't see any trees or ravens or mates. Jamieson saw nothing but blue sky below him for a long, long way. He was very dizzy and very scared.

Oh no, *he thought*. Where will I land?

The movie stopped. "Why did you stop it?" Xavion asked. "I want to know what happens."

"Your teacher's calling," said Jamieson. "We'll finish tomorrow. But be thinking. I don't want to miss Mum's grass cake with ketchup icing or all the pepperoni pizzas."

"Ok," Xavion said. "I'll be thinking. We've got to get you home... One more thing, Jamieson. Have you ever been to a carnival?"

"A carnival?" Jamieson said. "Let me —"

Then Jamieson imitated Mrs. Barnes.

"Xavion, wake up!" He sounded just like her.

Wait, that is Mrs. Barnes, Xavion thought. He looked around. He didn't see Jamieson anywhere.

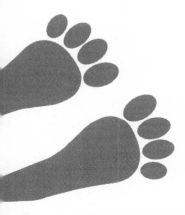

"Were you talking in your sleep again?" Mrs. Barnes asked.

Xavion didn't know why Mrs. Barnes always thought he was sleeping, but he didn't say a word. You could probably get in trouble for talking to kangaroos during time-out.

CHAPTER SIX

OH, SAY CAN YOU SEE ...

T he next day, Xavion packed Jamieson a snack. First, Xavion
cut a branch from his favorite climb-
ing tree. Then he grabbed a slice of
leftover pepperoni pizza from the
fridge.

Jamieson didn't know it, but
pepperoni pizza was Xavion's favorite food, too. Xavion knew his mom

had wondered why he hadn't eaten all his pizza at supper. She had even checked Xavion's temperature to see if he was sick. Xavion hadn't said a word.

When Xavion got to school, he noticed the red flag was still out. That meant no outside recess again. But Xavion didn't worry. He knew Jamieson would find him in the hall.

Time seemed to crawl that day. Austin and Chris were up to their old tricks. Whenever they passed by Jamieson's desk, they whispered the same old names — **"Bigfoot"** or **"Flapjack"**—nothing new.

Xavion ignored them. He couldn't risk being sent to the principal instead of time-out. He really needed to see Jamieson, so he could help him get home in time for his birthday.

Finally, time-out began. But, as usual, Jamieson was nowhere to be seen. And, once again, Xavion was getting sleepy.

Xavion had begun to snore when Jamieson tapped him on the shoulder.

"No time to talk today," Jamieson said. He handed Xavion a box of popcorn and grabbed the remote control. Xavion handed him the pizza and branch.

"Thanks, Xavion," Jamieson said. "I was getting hungry for something besides shrubs and popcorn."

"And rocks," Xavion said, laughing.

"And rocks," Jamieson agreed as he started the movie.

Jamieson was starting to fall from the sky when he noticed a giant goose flying toward him. As the goose flew closer, Jamieson noticed that the goose had windows — lots of windows.

That's not a goose, *thought Jamieson.* That's an airplane.

At first, Jamieson worried that

the airplane would fly right into him. He tried to jump out of the way, but jumping didn't work in the middle of the sky with nothing to bounce off. Then Jamieson tried to flap his arms, but without feathers and wings, that didn't work either.

Jamieson squinted his eyes and waited for the plane to hit him. But the plane didn't hit him. Instead, the nose of the plane whizzed by Jamieson.

Maybe, just maybe... *Jamieson thought.*

There was no time to finish the thought. Jamieson's instincts took over. He reached his right paw as high as he could — just like he would to slam-dunk a basketball.

When he felt something cold and metal hit his paw, he grabbed hold and pulled himself on top of the wing.

Whew, *he thought.* I made it.

But the plane kept flying. Jamieson began to think the plane would never stop. He clung for dear life to that airplane wing. Jamieson flew

through rain and lightning and hail. He passed over a huge ocean where he saw giant ships, schools of dolphins, and a whale. Jamieson felt tired and scared. The plane finally started to descend.

At last, *Jamieson thought.*

As the plane circled to land, he thought he saw the Statue of Liberty. He recognized it from a poster about countries of the world. Jamieson had taped the poster to his wall.

If that's the Statue of Liberty, *Jamieson thought,* I'm about to land a long, long way from home.

Jamieson stopped the movie.

"That's my story," Jamieson said. "When the plane got below the trees, I let go and bounced really high for a long time. Then I saw you playing basketball one day."

"You saw me?" Xavion asked.

"I did," Jamieson said. "You can jump really high, too!"

Xavion jumped a few times to show exactly how high he could jump.

"See," Jamieson said. "That's why I thought you could help me figure out how to bounce back home."

"I want to be home for my birthday."

Xavion told Jamieson to come to his house that night. Xavion sketched a map to his house and stuffed it into Jamieson's pouch.

"Why were you talking about a carnival?" Jamieson asked.

"Working on an idea," Xavion said. "We'll —"

"Xaaaviiooon!" said Mrs. Barnes. She was tapping his arm again. "You are a very deep sleeper."

Xavion still didn't know why Mrs. Barnes thought he was sleeping. But he didn't have time to wonder about that now. He had to help Jamieson get home.

CHAPTER SEVEN

XAVION'S PLAN

Xavion was drifting off to sleep when Jamieson sneaked into his room. Xavion had waited for hours for Jamieson, but Jamieson hadn't appeared. Xavion had spent the evening thinking about his plan. He had asked his mom a million questions about kangaroos.

"Why the sudden interest in kangaroos?" Xavion's mom had finally asked. "Is this homework?"

Xavion had decided not to talk about kangaroos any more. He didn't want his mom asking too many questions. He wasn't sure how she would react to him being in time-out or what she would think of a kangaroo named Jamieson. And the annual carnival started the next day.

If Xavion's mom grounded him, no way would he get to go.

Xavion already knew that his mom thought he was acting weird. Every time Xavion had tried to sneak something past her, she had seen him.

What's the plan?" Jamieson asked. "I'm ready to go home."

Xavion jumped straight up. "You scared me," he said.

"Didn't mean to, mate," Jamieson said. "Didn't realize you were asleep. No worries."

Xavion told Jamieson he had a plan to get Jamieson home in time for his birthday.

"Super," Jamieson said. "But where are all the trampolines?"

"We don't need any trampolines," Xavion said. "Jamieson, you're going home the same way you came — but on the inside of an airplane this time."

Jamieson's ears lifted.

Xavion pulled a piece of paper from beneath his pillow. The paper showed all the flights to Australia. Xavion had looked them up on the school computer during library hour. There was one flight the next day that would get Jamieson home in time for his birthday. Xavion had drawn a star beside it.

"Perfect, mate," Jamieson said. "I knew you'd figure something out."

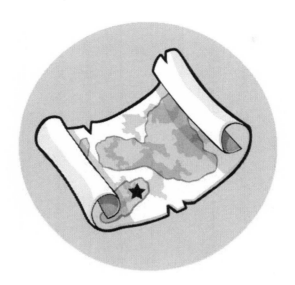

"There's a minor problem," Xavion said. "Well, actually two."

Jamieson's ears drooped.

"The airport is fifty miles from here," Xavion said. "And the ticket costs a lot. Like more than two years of allowance."

"I'll never get home," Jamieson said. His ears flopped. "Was that the whole plan?"

"That's not exactly the whole plan," Xavion said. "How do you feel about disguises?"

Xavion handed Jamieson a sweatshirt, some old sweatpants, and his old sneakers. Xavion had lots of old shoes because his feet kept growing.

"Try these on," Xavion said.

Jamieson took off his pouch. He pulled on the sweatshirt, then the sweatpants. Next, he laced up the shoes.

Xavion took the old mop head his mom had been about to throw out and put it on Jamieson's head. Then he put a baseball cap on top. Finally, Xavion handed Jamieson a pair of sunglasses to wear.

"Now put on your pack," Xavion said. "I mean your pouch. But wear it on your back this time."

"OK," Jamieson said. "But wearing a pouch on your back is really weird."

"I think you'll pass," Xavion said.

"Pass for what?" Jamieson asked.

"You'll see tomorrow," Xavion said. "Like the chief raven said: Just be ready for the jump of your life."

"Uh-oh," said Jamieson.

Xavion was so excited that night that he couldn't sleep. Or he thought he couldn't sleep.

"Wake up, mate," Jamieson said. "It's time to go!" Xavion looked at the clock – it was already 10:45 a.m. and the carnival started at 11. He had overslept again. He liked to sleep really late on Saturdays.

Xavion dressed while Jamieson put on his disguise.

"Let's go," Xavion said.

The screen door slammed on their way out. "Where are you headed?" Xavion's mom called.

Busted, thought Xavion. *Game over*.

"To the carnival," Xavion said.

"Ok," his mom said. "You know the rules. Straight there and straight back. I'm watching."

"And ask first next time."

"Yes, ma'am."

Luckily, his mom hadn't seen Jamieson.

The carnival set up each year in an open lot across the street from Xavion's house. Xavion loved the carnival — the cotton candy, the rides, the lights, and music. He especially loved the games and the prizes.

Last year, he had won two goldfish by bouncing ping-pong balls into bowls.

Today, he would have to focus. He and Jamieson were there for one game and one game only.

Xavion pointed to a sign that said World's Greatest Bounce Off. Behind the sign was a trampoline. About twenty feet above the trampoline were some small stuffed animals. There were puppies, bears, and unicorns. The higher you jumped, the bigger the prizes became. And about half a football field above the trampoline was a huge, shiny, gold bell.

The sign said it all:

Ring the bell and win an all-expenses paid trip to anywhere in the world.

TICKETS $5

"If you ring the bell," Xavion said, "You could use the trip to go home."

"Hitting the bell will be a piece of cake," Jamieson said. "Especially compared to the last jump!"

Xavion didn't know of any rules banning kangaroos from playing the game. But he wasn't certain and thought Jamieson should wear a disguise anyway.

People weren't used to seeing kangaroos at the carnival. Or anywhere else, really.

"But we don't have five dollars," Jamieson said.

"We do," Xavion said. "We actually had ten dollars and fifty cents, but I had to split it with the crows.

"And I used a quarter to buy some gum."

Xavion explained how he had made a deal with the crows.

"They didn't try to trick you?" Jamieson asked.

"These crows were really nice," Xavion said. "They kept their word."

Xavion said his deal with the crows worked like this: The crows brought Xavion any aluminum cans they saw scattered around town.

Then, Xavion smashed the cans with his big feet and put them in a bag. When he had a bag full, he took it to the recycling center and exchanged the cans for cash. He split the cash with the crows. It had taken seven bags to get enough money.

"Good thinking," Jamieson said.

"Thanks," Xavion said. "Now, let's go. You just make sure your ears stay under that hat."

Xavion handed Jamieson the five dollars and pointed him toward the two men running the game.

Jamieson bounced as softly as he could toward the men.

"One ticket to ring the bell, please, mate," Jamieson said as he handed over the five dollars.

"Mate?" the older man said as he looked closely at Jamieson. Jamieson pulled his cap down lower on his head.

Busted, thought Xavion.

103

"I mean sir," Jamieson quickly corrected.

"Good luck ringing the bell," the older man said. He handed Jamieson the ticket.

"You'll need it," the younger worker said. Both men laughed.

Jamieson walked to Xavion and handed him his pouch to hold while he jumped.

"Let's do this," Jamieson said.

"Let's do this." Xavion pushed Jamieson's cap even farther down on his head.

The two men running the game reclined in their patio chairs. Jamieson climbed onto the trampoline. One of the men dozed. *I'd sleep, too,* Xavion thought. *No one has ever rung that bell.*

Jamieson warmed up with a few low, slow bounces. He swung his arms back and forth to loosen up. After that, he rose higher and higher with each bounce. He didn't reach for any of the smaller stuffed animals. He didn't even reach for the stuffed alligator or the stuffed kangaroo.

"Two more jumps!" Xavion shouted. "You'll have it!"

One more jump. Jamieson whizzed by hundreds of stuffed animals. He flew by a stuffed raven.

Another jump, and then Jamieson rang the bell.

The bell was super loud — a million times louder than when Xavion had called Austin four-eyes.

The men running the game fell out of their chairs at the sound.

A crowd gathered and started to cheer. A reporter from the local TV station wanted an interview. Jamieson basked in the glory until Xavion pulled his arm.

"We've got to go, mate," Xavion

said. "Your birthday. Remember? The airport is 50 miles away, and your plane leaves in two hours."

Jamieson shook a few hands, took a few photos with the crowd, and collected the prize. Jamieson and Xavion were almost to the carnival entrance when Xavion heard them.

"Hey, Flapjack," Austin called. "What's your buddy's name? Sasquatch Senior? His feet are even bigger than yours."

Xavion did not need this right now.

"And look at those ears!" Chris said. "You've got kangaroo ears!"

Unfortunately, Jamieson's ears had slipped out from under the cap. The neighborhood kids were starting to gather.

"Well, actually, mate, you're very observant," Jamieson said. "I am actually a kanga—"

Xavion elbowed Jamieson in the ribs to stop him from admitting he was a kangaroo.

"What'd you go and do that for, mate?" Jamieson asked.

Before Xavion could answer, a dark cloud descended on the crowd. Then the cloud began to flap.

And croak.

And caw.

That's not a cloud, thought Xavion. *It's the crows.*

One crow snatched Austin's hat off his head and flew away. Another grabbed Chris's cap. Austin, Chris, and the other kids ran after the crows and the hats.

The chief crow flew down to Xavi-on and Jamieson.

"Thanks, chief," Xavion said.

"You fellas, I mean, mates, better get a move on," the chief crow said. "One of you has a plane to catch."

"Your crows are way nicer than my ravens," Jamieson said.

"Agreed!" said Xavion.

The two reached Xavion's front door.

"Now what?" Jamieson asked.

"Here comes the hard part," Xavion said. "My mom will have to drive us to the airport."

"What do you think she'll say?" Jamieson asked.

Xavion gave him an I-have-no-clue shrug.

Xavion walked through the front door and looked at his mom. She was reading a magazine.

"Mum," Xavion began. "I was wondering—"

His mom held up her hand to stop him. "Did you just call me 'mum'?" she asked. "Xavion, what is going on with you?"

So, Xavion told her the story—the whole story, even the parts when Jamieson didn't listen to his mum. He even told the part about being in time-out.

"We'll talk about that later," Xavion's mom said. Her face looked stern. "For now, let's find Jamieson, so we can take him to the airport."

"He's pretty easy to find," Xavion said. "He's right here." Jamieson hopped in from the porch.

Xavion's mom gave Jamieson a great, big hug. Jamieson's eyes filled with tears.

"None of that now," Xavion's mom said. "We've got to hurry to catch the plane."

CHAPTER EIGHT

TIME'S UP IN TIME-OUT

Xavion didn't hear from Jamieson at all the rest of that day. Xavion had hoped Jamieson would call when he landed in Australia. On Monday, Xavion went to school. There were no signs of Jamieson there, either.

Xavion worried that Jamieson hadn't gotten home. Xavion's mom had taken them to the airport in plenty of time. So, Jamieson should have made it home for his birthday. But there was always the chance that Jamieson had talked to the ravens again.

At recess time, Mrs. Barnes called Xavion to her desk. "Xavion," Mrs. Barnes said. "You've been so good in class and in time-out. Have fun at recess today."

"OK," Xavion said. He hung his head as he walked to the playground.

"You don't seem too happy," Mrs. Barnes said. "I thought you would be excited to play basketball again. After all, when you were in time-out last week, you slept the whole time."

Xavion couldn't imagine why Mrs.

Barnes thought he had been sleeping. And he was still amazed that she had not seen Jamieson. Maybe teachers didn't have eyes in the backs of their heads after all.

Jamieson walked onto the playground. That's when Austin and Chris started in about Xavion's big feet again. The other kids crowded round.

It didn't bother Xavion at all. His big feet are what made him such a good jumper. And that's why Jamieson had found him.

Xavion's face didn't turn red.

Xavion didn't call Austin four-eyes.

Nothing to see here, people, thought Xavion. *Move along.*

The other kids walked away, and

Austin and Chris eventually, more or less, left Xavion alone.

That night, Xavion was almost asleep when he heard Jamieson's voice on the telephone. *That's weird,* Xavion thought. *I didn't even hear the phone ring.*

"G'day, mate," Jamieson said.

"G'day, Jamieson," Xavion said, even though it was night. "Did you get your prize and your grass cake?"

"All of the above," Jamieson said. "I hold the official world record for highest jumping kangaroo. Plus, I got another medal for longest-jumping kangaroo. And, I got a special award for kangaroo that flew the longest on an airplane's wing.

"I also got a warning to never do any of those things again."

"What about the pepperoni pizzas?" asked Xavion.

"They're delicious," said Jamieson. "I left a slice underneath your pillow. Grab it, and let's watch the rest of the movie."

Xavion found the pizza, picked out a few leaves and rocks, and lay back to watch the movie on the ceiling.

When Jamieson stepped off the airplane, his family was thrilled to see him. They hugged and laughed and cried. They were so happy, in

fact, that they forgot that Jamieson was in trouble for listening to the ravens. Jamieson hoped they would never remember.

That night, Jamieson's friends and family celebrated his birthday. They ate a giant grass cake with ketchup icing.

Then they ate pepperoni pizza — the first of the million pizzas that

Jamieson and the ravens had won. Jamieson split the prize with the ravens, even though they had tricked him.

"A promise is a promise," his dad had said.

When Jamieson woke up the next morning, his mum still hadn't said anything about being in trouble.

Whew, *Jamieson thought.* I'm in the clear.

But that morning, as Jamieson and his mum stepped outside, a raven croaked.

"Hey, Jamieson," the raven began. "How was that last jump?"

Jamieson ignored him. He definitely wouldn't talk to ravens anymore. Jamieson hoped his mum

123

hadn't heard the raven.

His mum stopped in her tracks.

"That's how this all started," his mum said.

"What started?" Jamieson asked, hoping to change the subject. "Another good day with my mum?"

Jamieson's attempt failed.

"Now, I remember," his mum said. "And I have an idea."

Jamieson worried. This was not sounding good.

"To help you remember not to talk to the ravens," his mum said, "I'll see if your teacher will put you in time-out for a week."

Xavion stopped the movie. "Aw, man!" Xavion said. "That's harsh."

"I know," Jamieson said. "And I get so bored in time-out. Sometimes I even fall asleep. Will you come visit me?"

"I will," Xavion said. "Just about the time you're drifting off to sleep, I'll tap you on the shoulder, and we'll have another adventure."

"Sounds great," Jamieson said.

"OK," Xavion said. "See you tomorrow."

"Until then, mate," said Jamieson.

The next morning, Xavion ran out of his bedroom.

"Mum, guess what—" Xavion began.

His mom interrupted.

"Did you call me 'mum', Xavion?" she asked. "What has gotten into you?"

"Remember when the phone rang last night?" Xavion asked. "That was Jamieson."

"The phone didn't ring last night," Xavion's mom said. "And who is this Jamieson person?"

Xavion started to remind his mom

about how she drove Jamieson to the airport. He started to remind her of the whole story and how Jamieson wasn't a person but a kangaroo. But that meant he would have to remind her that he had been in time-out all week. And that might mean more trouble.

"Never mind," Xavion said. "Just wondering if we could have grass cake with ketchup icing for my next birthday. That's all."

Xavion walked outside. A crow cawed in the distance.

ONCE AN AWARD-WINNING NEWSPAPER
COLUMNIST AND FREELANCE WRITER,
M.L. FLURRY HAS NEVER CROSSED
PATHS WITH A KANGAROO BUT
HOPES TO ONE DAY

Made in the USA
Lexington, KY
06 December 2019